Ana Aranda

OUR DAY OF THE DEAD CELEBRATION

NANCY PAULSEN BOOKS

To my father, with all my love forever.
Thank you for the happiest memories
and experiences in life.

NANCY PAULSEN BOOKS
An imprint of Penguin Random House LLC, New York

First published in the United States of America by Nancy Paulsen Books,
an imprint of Penguin Random House LLC, 2022

Copyright © 2022 by Ana Aranda

Visit us online at penguinrandomhouse.com

Library of Congress Cataloging-in-Publication Data
Names: Aranda, Ana, author, illustrator. • Title: Our Day of the Dead celebration / Ana Aranda.
Description: New York: Nancy Paulsen Books, 2022. • Includes author's note.
Summary: "A family honors their living and dead relatives as they celebrate the Day of the Dead
with shared food and stories"—Provided by publisher. • Identifiers: LCCN 2022006787
ISBN 9780525514282 (hardcover) • ISBN 9780525514312 (ebook) • ISBN 9780525514299 (ebook)
Subjects: CYAC: All Souls' Day—Fiction. • Family life—Fiction. • LCGFT: Picture books.
Classification: LCC PZ7.1.A722 Ou 2022 • DDC [E]—dc23
LC record available at https://lccn.loc.gov/2022006787

Manufactured in Italy
ISBN 9780525514282
1 3 5 7 9 10 8 6 4 2
LEG

Edited by Nancy Paulsen • Art directed by Cecilia Yung
Design by Nicole Rheingans • Text set in Andes Neue
The art was done in watercolor, inks, gouache,
and a little bit of Himalayan salt on watercolor paper.

FAMILIA DEL FARO

TENORIO · DELIA · JULIETA

ABUELITA · RAMÓN · GRANDMA · GRANDPA

AMALIA · PATY · LUCHA · MOM · DAD · VALERIO

LUIS · PEPE · CLAUDIA · BETO · PAZ · MAR

Today is the Day of the Dead!
It is a happy day when
we celebrate with our family.

There is a lot to do to get ready.
We go to the market to pick the brightest
marigolds and some sugar skulls.

Everyone is coming to our house.
The living and the dead! Grandma told
us that this is the time when the spirits
of the departed come back to visit.

We decorate sugar skulls for all the relatives we miss.

Mom is teaching us to cook Aunt Lucha's favorite dish—sweet tamales.

Tía Lucha keeps bees and eats five tamales
with honey every morning.
She is the sweetest person I know!

My sister, Paz, is practicing the accordion.

It belonged to our great-grandfather Tenorio.

He used to play all over the country.

Abuelita's husband, Grandpa Ramón, liked
to travel, too, and spoke eight languages. He visited
every continent in search of rare objects and stories.
He kept track of his adventures in his journals.

For dessert, Dad is teaching us how to make our family's famous soft almond cookies.

Now our food, flowers, and sugar skulls
are ready for the altar. Paz writes a poem for
Great-grandfather Tenorio, to add to the altar:

NOW THAT YOU ARE AWAY,
YOUR ACCORDION ASKED ME TO PLAY
THE MOST BEAUTIFUL SONG
TO KEEP YOUR MEMORY STRONG.

And I write one for Grandpa Ramón:

WE MISS YOU AND YOUR SNEEZE.
DID IT REALLY ALMOST BLOW DOWN SOME TREES?

Everything is ready—but we need the guests!
Waiting is hard! So I write one more poem
for Great-grandma Delia, who was an artist.

YOUR FAVORITE COLOR WAS GREEN,
THE BEST COLOR EVER SEEN.
YOU LOVED THE SPRING
AND BIRDS THAT SING.

And then, *hooray!* They are here.

Claudia is an artist and draws pictures
on the patio of all the places
Grandpa Ramón told us about.

We are all getting hungry but must wait
for our most important guest.
Finally, the one who knows
all the family stories arrives.

My family loves to be together. We sing and dance to celebrate our family. We feel close to everyone—the living and the dead.

At dinner, Abuelita tells stories,
and we could listen forever.

When the party is over,

we are sad to say goodbye.

But we are all happy we had a day
to remember. Just like we have
loved ones we will never, ever forget.

Author's Note

Since ancient times, humans have sought ways to celebrate the lives of their family members who died. In Mexico, some people celebrate their departed loved ones by making altars. They can be decorated with sugar skulls, marigold flowers, beloved food, and pan de muerto, which is a traditional bread made for this season. Sharing stories and writing poems, called **calaveras** (which translates as "skulls"), about the dead also help keep their memories alive. In this book, you'll find a story inspired by my family, who loves to remember the sweet times we had with those who are no longer with us. It is important to remember, because when we remember, we live again, and they live again through us.

-ANA